Eli and Uncle Dawn

Liz Rosenberg • Susan Gaber

HARCOURT BRACE & COMPANY

San Diego   New York   London

Requests for permission to make copies of any part
of the work should be mailed to: Permissions Department,
Harcourt Brace & Company, 6277 Sea Harbor Drive,
Orlando, Florida 32887-6777.

Library of Congress Cataloging-in-Publication Data
Rosenberg, Liz.
Eli and Uncle Dawn/Liz Rosenberg;
illustrated by Susan Gaber. — 1st ed.
p. cm.
Summary: With the help of his magician uncle,
a young boy finds his special toy elephant.
ISBN 0-15-200947-7
[1. Uncles—Fiction. 2. Toys—Fiction. 3. Magicians—Fiction.]
I. Gaber, Susan, ill. II. Title.
PZ7.R71894El 1997
[E]—dc20   95-22927

First edition
A C E F D B

Printed in Singapore

The illustrations in this book were done in watercolor,
acrylic, and colored pencil on Coquille board.
The display type was hand-lettered by
Georgia Deaver, based on Susan Gaber's design.
The text type was set in Adroit Light.
Color separations by Bright Arts, Ltd., Singapore
Printed and bound by Tien Wah Press, Singapore
This book was printed on totally
chlorine-free Nymolla Matte Art paper.
Production supervision by Stanley Redfern
and Pascha Gerlinger
Designed by Camilla Filancia

For Eli, of course—
and his magical uncles
and aunts and cousins
—L. R.

For Aunt Sylvia,
Aunt Rita, Uncle Leon,
Gloria, and Abe
—S. G.

Eli lived in a big stone house, in a room with a small bay window. He had a mother and a father, and an elephant named George, who went with him everywhere.

His uncle Dawn lived upstairs, in a sunny room that had once been the attic.

Uncle Dawn was a magician, and a handyman on the side. He made a special blue shade for Eli's bay window, to keep out the drafts. On windy nights it fluttered and billowed like a sail. Eli and George, lying cozily underneath, would play that their bed was a giant ship.

Eli's father offered Uncle Dawn a real job at the downtown office.

"Magic is real," said Uncle Dawn, pulling a handful of flowers out of the sugar bowl.

Eli's father only frowned.

One afternoon Uncle Dawn took Eli and George
for a picnic lunch. Eli and George shared, as usual.
George liked peanuts and Eli liked bananas, so
they ate peanut-butter-and-banana sandwiches.
Uncle Dawn had three hard-boiled eggs, two pickles,
a bottle of milk, and an orange.

After lunch he made the tablecloth disappear. Then,
magically, he turned into a ferocious grizzly bear and
chased Eli through the woods. Eli caught him and tamed
him, and rode him home just in time for supper....

But they forgot about George.

Eli remembered the minute they sat down to eat.

He rushed to the front porch, but his parents said it was too dark to see.

"George is out there somewhere," said Eli unhappily.

"We'll look first thing in the morning," his mother promised. "Now eat your supper."

But Eli couldn't. So Uncle Dawn carried him piggyback up to his room. He showed him the best card tricks ever and taught Eli how to whistle loudly by blowing between his thumbs.

"Do you think George can hear us whistle?" asked Eli.

"I'm sure of it," said Uncle Dawn. "Now try to get some sleep."

Outside, leaves scraped against the gravel. The geese honked good-bye, heading south. All Eli could think about was George, all alone out there in the dark.

The wind howled, rattling the glass. Eli's shade fluttered and flapped. It blew off the window and hung above his bed, puffed out with wind. Eli grabbed hold and floated out into the night.

He sailed past the window to the room where his mother
and father lay reading in bed. He drifted over a pond, where
the tops of the waves wet the bottoms of his feet. Then he
steered between dark trees, tilting the blue shade this way
and that, heading into the deepest part of the woods.

The wind died down and Eli landed. He spotted an
orange peel left over from his lunch and put it in his
pajama pocket. It was dark in the woods. There were
strange soft noises all around him. Something gleamed
in the low branches of a tree.... A pair of bright eyes—
it was George!

They were overjoyed to see each other.

"I heard you whistling," said George.

The woods rustled behind them. A branch snapped, and suddenly a huge bear lumbered into the clearing.

Eli knew right away it was Uncle Dawn.

"Is George all right?" asked Uncle Dawn. He lightly thumped the elephant's chest and peered into his ears. Then he looked at Eli and frowned. "What are *you* doing out of bed?" he asked.

Before Eli could explain, the shade filled again with wind. It pulled him up, up through the trees.

Uncle Dawn was left below, holding George. "We'll meet you back home!" he called.

Eli sailed out of the woods. He skimmed over the public library, the baseball field, and the town clock. He coasted over the roofs of his friends' houses.

Eli landed in his bed just as his parents walked into his room.

"Can't sleep?" his mother asked. "Still worrying about George?"

"Not to worry," said Uncle Dawn. He sat in the rocking chair, holding the elephant.

"It's George! Thank goodness! But how on earth—?" cried Eli's mother. Even his father looked impressed.

Eli smiled and sat up straighter in bed. "Uncle Dawn is a true magician," he said.

"Magic," said Uncle Dawn shyly. "It's a funny thing."

He produced a tablecloth from behind Eli's ear, and together they all had a delicious midnight snack—including peanut-butter-and-banana sandwiches, which Eli and George shared, as usual.